Murder Under Glass

By

Cassandra Knight

Dedication:

For Becca, who liked to write stories

Table of Contents

Acknowledgements:

Thanks are due to always my children, whose energy and authenticity are my continuing inspiration. Thanks also to my mother, who never gives up, and my friends, and last but not least thank you to Andrew, without whose steady companionship I would be lost.

Chapter 1:
The Man with the Practiced Smile

Ted Omen smiled.

It was the kind of smile that belonged in a catalogue for expensive cosmetic dentistry or crypto investments. Wide. Flashy. Practiced. His lips moved upward, but his eyes didn't bother to play along. They were cold, light grey, and flat as a concrete sky. Not hostile. Just not part of the performance. His hair was, however, carefully tousled, elegantly highlighted, almost imperceptibly, but the product of hours of careful attention.

Prohibition era jazz bring played live-in Zoe's Lounge spilled from a grand piano under the stained-glass dome like molasses on silver. Some trio from Montreal was playing something smooth and forgettable, the kind of music that made people think they were richer than they were. In the corner, behind a cut-glass tumbler of Scotch that cost more than George Jeremiah's well-worn shoes, Ted Omen was holding court.

George sat opposite him in a chair that had been reupholstered more times than most marriages. He was a small man, deliberately so. Soft voice, unremarkable suit, a pen that didn't click. George was the kind of reporter you never remembered until your name showed up in his article and you had to call your lawyer.

Ted didn't notice the quiet ones. They bored him.

"Picture it," Ted said, spreading his arms like he was revealing a kingdom and not just slinging another bad idea in a good suit. "A casino. But not just any casino. An AI-integrated, fully immersive, next-generation entertainment temple. On the very edge of the Ridea Falls, George blinked, "'Temple?" Ted grinned, "Why not think big? Ottawa is the capital of a G7 country. We need to stop thinking small. We've got the land, we've got the investors. Hell, I've already got two venture capitalists out of San Francisco practically begging to get in on it. Imagine robot croupiers, blackjack tables run by machine learning algorithms. Facial recognition for drink preferences. No mistakes. No unions. No drama."

George tapped his pen against his notepad, a subtle metronome under the piano's drifting chords. "So, no job creation, and no ecological considerations, either. The FallsMinder group says the project could endanger the entire riparian ecosystem."

Ted leaned back and scoffed. "FallsMinder is a gaggle of old granola hobbyists with a website and too much time. You know what's endangered, George? The city's economy. Downtown's still gasping for air. We have six times as many homeless people per capita as any other city in Canada, and they are gathered together on our tourist sites. This project is a defibrillator. Ottawa is a withered old shell of its Gothic glory. We need an influx of tourists, and of new sources of funds in this city. I'm not just proposing a casino—I'm offering salvation."

George raised a brow. "The National Capital Commission hasn't approved your plans."

Ted waved the air like it had personally disappointed him. "The NCC is ceremonial. Their job is to fret about flag colours and bicycle paths. I briefed Environment Minister Andrew Jones-Middleton last week—he gets it."

"Minister Jones-Middleton hasn't made a statement; the project is not yet approved."

Ted's smile shrank slightly, sharpening at the edges. "He will. When the time is right. I don't pressure people, George. I just make things so obvious they stop pretending to need convincing."

"Like you made it obvious to the Algonquin communities that they didn't need to be consulted?"

That got a pause. A flicker, just a hitch in the blink rate. Then the grin returned, lacquered back into place. "We're planning a cultural outreach strategy. It's all part of Phase Two. But let's not pretend we're building a pipeline through the Amazon. This is a casino. There's already a city here. Nobody's carving up sacred land."

George nodded slowly and wrote nothing down. "Ted," said George a bit softly, "   You are aware of course that the general counsel for the

Fallsminder group is not just any lawyer but in fact your own former wife, Tatiana Goode-Omen? Any personal grudges motivating your ambition?"

Ted smiled even more broadly, "Well now, George, they always say Ottawa is a small town. If it comes to it, and they raise a ruckus about our innovation, if they try to stop progress, it won't be the first time I see Tatiana in court."

"So you're saying you are looking for a fight?", said George, provocatively.

"Of course not," Ted chuckled slightly, "but I won't let my personal history stand in the way of the greatness, of the impact, of the tremendous potential, of this project. If small-minded, parochial hippies can't get on board with that vision, then they will have to be dealt with." He smiled once more, and his teeth looked rather sharp.

When the interview wrapped, Ted stood first. He extended his hand, a long-fingered, skeletal thing with perfectly buffed nails and knuckles like expensive coat hangers. George took it out of professional instinct, but the sensation stopped him cold.

The hand was almost weightless. All bone, no substance. A hand made for empty gestures. In that moment, George saw him clearly—not the shark or the wolf, but something worse: a mannequin with a tape recorder for a voice. An empty suit filled with big words and bigger voids.

Ted turned toward the bar, toward the mirrors, toward the polished brass and soft leather, where his reflection would lie to him the same way he lied to everyone else. He walked like a man who had never once considered he might fall.

George remained seated. He watched Ted vanish into the bar's golden haze, watched the piano player's fingers spill silk into the air.

The Château Laurier glowed like a Gothic dream from another century. High ceilings, chandeliers the size of moonlight, and windows that caught the Parliament buildings like a postcard pressed in glass. The walls whispered old power—colonial, white, and untouched by the kind of corruption that made headlines because it was too boring to be sexy.

Zoe's Lounge was filled with money and the ghosts of men who once had too much of it. George closed his notebook and slipped it into his coat.

After an hour spent in close quarters with Ted Omen, George craved some fresh air.

George didn't believe in ghosts. But he did believe in telling the truth. And he would be writing a story, he resolved, as he stepped out of the Chateau Laurier onto Wellington Street, into the blustery fall afternoon.

The Château Laurier sat at the lip of the Rideau Canal like a dowager queen in mourning—draped in limestone, too proud to crumble, too dignified to smile. Built when Canada was still trying to impress the British Empire and herself, the hotel had the ambition of a railway baron's mistress and the bones of a Scottish fortress. It opened in 1912 with fresh stone, French linens, and one notable absence: its patron, Charles Melville Hays, who'd gone down with the Titanic before he could see his empire crowned in copper. The place was always touched by ghosts after that political ones, imperial ones, and the kind that smoke cigars no one can smell.

Somewhere inside, tucked among the portraits of prime ministers and rotarians, hung the one of Winston Churchill. Or rather, it used to. The only portrait he ever sat for in Canada vanished sometime between the last bellboy's wink and the latest federal scandal. Stolen, maybe. Lost, more likely. But no one ever looked too hard. The hotel didn't need the portrait to remember him. The whole place already smelled like a war room: thick carpets, darker secrets, and the lingering impression that power was something you wore in your coat lining. The Château was where deals were whispered and careers buried, all under chandeliers the size of regrets.

The wind came off the river like it had a grudge. It rattled the red and yellow maple leaves down Sussex Drive in nervous little bunches, their scuttling echoing the steps of bureaucrats headed home from work, the wind and the growing dusk chasing them east past government stone and wrought iron fences. Walking that stretch in late October meant buttoning your coat high and keeping your head low—especially if you had anything to regret. The Château Laurier receded behind you like an old lady in a beautiful dress. Ahead, embassies stood like bored sentries, each window blank and watching. The American flag flapped hard against its pole like it was looking for someone to slap. Across the street, the Global Affairs building loomed like a mausoleum for forgotten diplomacy—long, grey, and dignified in that Canadian way that always felt a little ashamed of itself.

The road curved north and then east again, drawing you out toward the suburbs of the city, turning from Sussex Drive into Rockcliffee Parkway, where the river stops pretending to behave. The Rideau Falls don't roar like Niagara, they seethe. Two wide sheets of water, twin veils pulled from the brow of the Ottawa River, tumbling fifty feet into a stone throat. In the summer season, a jaunty café sits beside them, the Tavern on the Falls, all shut up and gloomy now in the fading light of windy autumn dusk.

The mist rose in ghostly gusts, catching in the bronze folds of the war memorial and the steel bones of the Minto bridges nearby. On days like this, the air was all river cold, metallic, and old enough to remember when this land answered to no one. You could stand there and listen to the water punch through time. Some said it was beautiful. Others said it was sacred.

George stood on the bridge overlooking the falls, next to the offices of Canadian Geographic, startled and unsurprised that Ted Omen looked at all this and saw a casino.

Chapter 2
Ghost

The day had the bright-eyed clarity of someone trying to make up for past mistakes. Sunlight fell hard on the red-brick houses of Sandy Hill, catching on frost-glazed eavestroughs and bouncing off the windshields of parallel-parked Subarus like diamonds in pawnshop glass. The air was sharp, clean, and impatient—an Ottawa wind that knew winter was coming and wanted to sweep the stage before it arrived. Trees rattled their bare limbs in protest, and somewhere overhead a parliament of crows screamed at nothing in particular.

Inside the FallsMinder offices, the radiator clanked like a haunted typewriter. The place was a Victorian holdover—three floors of creaking floorboards, crown moulding, and mismatched furniture donated by people who still thought landlines meant permanence. The house smelled like brewed coffee, dog fur, printer toner, and a faint trace of eucalyptus from someone's well-meaning diffuser. Tatiana stood near the big front window, bathed in the morning sun that filtered through gauzy linen curtains, one hand resting lightly on the golden head of her retriever, Ghost, who lay sprawled like a hearthrug across the oriental carpet.

The dog lifted his eyes briefly as the front door banged open with the force of a scandal.

"Have you read it?" came the voice—part fury, part panic.

Marieve Dumont entered like a thunderclap in cashmere. Silver hair swept back like she'd just stepped off a wind tunnel, coat unbuttoned, the Ottawa Citizen rolled under one arm like she meant to beat someone with it. She was sixty, maybe a touch over, and she moved with the kind of authority that made interns scramble and politicians backpedal.

Tatiana didn't flinch. "Of course I read it," she said, without turning around. "Online. At six-thirty. Right after Ghost decided the world needed him to bark at a squirrel."

Marieve let out a breath that sounded like it had been held since 1998. "It's outrageous. He calls it a temple. Like he's building the Parthenon and not a chrome nightmare on sacred water."

"He believes his own bullshit,",said Tatiana calmly," I learned that a long time ago. He is not exactly lying, because it is a delusional truth. They call it confabulating," Tatiana turned. "It's bluster. There are layers of legal approvals. NCC, environmental review, heritage consultations. And the Minister—Jones-Middleton—he's coming to the gala tonight."

Marieve dropped the newspaper on the nearest table. George Jeremiah's article glared up from the front page like a man smirking at his own cleverness. "You really think he'll stop it?"

Tatiana reached for her coffee. It was cold. "I think we remind him what he said last election about stewardship and climate leadership. I think we remind him tonight, under fairy lights and biodegradable cutlery and with five hundred donors watching and TV cameras behind them. We remind him he works for the people, and the people need environmental conservation."

A creak came from upstairs. Someone laughed in the kitchen. Somewhere behind them, a kettle whistled like a distant train.

Outside, the bright fall light slanted across Laurier Avenue like a stage cue. The wind blew hopeful and hard. Tatiana looked down at Ghost, who blinked once and thumped his tail. She smiled, faintly.

"It won't be the first time I squared off legally against Ted Omen," Tatiana said. "And he found the last instance very expensive, didn't he?" Ghost's tail wagged as if to signify agreement.

Chapter 3
Black Widower

Tatiana stood in the deep bay window of her red brick century home, overlooking the calm bend of Patterson's Creek, a small offshoot of the Rideau Canal. Golden light from the setting sun dappled the water, where ducks left slow, perfect ripples in their wake. The house wrapped around her like an old wool shawl—worn, softened, and deeply known. Its creaks were the language of comfort, not complaint. It was the one place in the world that had always been hers, in every sense that mattered.

Three generations of her family had lived here, ever since her grandfather came to Ottawa as a research scientist for the National Research Council. She had taken her first steps on these oak floors, and later watched her own children do the same. After her parents died—her father Ivan of heart disease, and her mother Titania of cancer two years later—Tatiana, an only child, had inherited both the house and the tidy, surprising fortune that came with it. She'd thought, in those early days of mourning, that she'd be swallowed by the quiet. But instead, the house had held her. Its wide rooms, high ceilings, and lingering smell of beeswax and old books became her anchor.

Ted Omen came into her life not long after her mother's funeral. She met him at university. He was dazzling then—or at least dazzling enough. There were happy years, certainly. Their early days were filled with optimism: a new venture for him, a growing family, sunlight on fresh-painted nursery walls. She offered her legal expertise freely, not noticing at first how seamlessly it served his ambitions. Later, with clarity earned the hard way, she realized how precisely he had timed his arrival—right when grief made her generous and unguarded.

The triplets came first: a whirlwind of girlhood and colour and love. Then Wolfgang, born a few years later. A surprise, and a strain. Pre-eclampsia had nearly ended her life. The condition, coupled with the closeness of the pregnancies, left her heart permanently weakened—a quiet fact she carried like a locked drawer inside her chest. Years later, one of the girls would text her in a moment of sibling debate: No, Mom wasn't the

Black Widow. She didn't kill Dad. Medically—slowly—in fact, because he made her pregnant, in a sense, he was killing her. He was the Black Widower.

Wolfgang was stretched out on the couch now, long legs crossed at the ankle, his hair still damp from the shower. Tatiana, standing at her vanity, fastened an earring and caught his eye in the mirror.

"I don't want to go," he muttered. "It's going to be lame. I'll be the only kid there."

Rather than push, Tatiana opened her phone and started a FaceTime call. A second later, Freya, Erinye, and Ariadne tumbled into view from their respective dorm rooms—talking over one another, laughing, full of conspiratorial glee.

"Oh come on, Wolf," said Freya. "You know Mom's going to be the only one there without a date and without any of her kids."

Wolfgang sighed, " you twits all abandoned me when you went away to university."

"You're her only date now," Erinye added. "She needs backup."

"Besides," Ariadne chimed in, "make it a social experiment. Who wears cufflinks anymore? Observe. Take notes."

Wolfgang rolled his eyes but smiled faintly. He sat up and wandered off in the direction of his closet.

As the girls turned their attention to their mother, Freya tilted her head. "You look nice, Mom."

"Very elegant," said Ariadne.

"Now all you need is a handsome stranger to ask you to dance," Erinye added.

Tatiana arched an eyebrow. "I am attending this for business reasons. A woman doesn't need to be married to be happy. Or partnered. Or even have children, for that matter. It's a perfectly acceptable ending to be alone."

Freya smirked. "Sure, sure. Just say you're happy we exist."

"Yeah," Erinye chimed in. "Reassure your children that you don't regret giving us life."

Tatiana laughed, but then her voice softened. "Having you four… was the most important thing I've ever done. And the best. No regrets. Not for a second."

The line went quiet for a beat, and then Ariadne grinned. "Remember when she used to tell us ghost stories before bed?"

"Of course," said Freya. "The dog is literally named Ghost."

From the hallway, Ghost—a very dignified golden retriever with greying whiskers—gave a soft woof in response, as if acknowledging the tribute.

Tatiana smiled and leaned a little closer to the camera. "Want to hear one for old time's sake?"

The girls nodded eagerly. "Always."

"There's a local story," Tatiana said, her voice slipping into the low, steady cadence they all knew from childhood, "about a woman who lived by the Ottawa River, long ago—Algonquin, some say. She fell in love with a man who promised to meet her one night, by moonlight, to paddle south together to a new life. But he never came. Some say he changed his mind. Others say he never meant to be there at all. Either way, he was a trickster. Heartbroken, she stepped into her canoe alone, and paddled under the stars until she reached the Rideau Falls. And there, she let the water take her. On clear nights, people still say they can see her—long hair flowing behind her like riverweed, canoe cutting a silent path through the mist."

The girls were quiet, a little spooked, a little moved.

"That is sad," said Erinye softly.

Then Ariadne checked the time and gave a pointed look. "You'd better go, Mom. You're going to be late."

Downstairs, Wolfgang called up that he was ready. Tatiana took one last glance at her daughters on the screen—her heart, her chaos, her joy—then turned off the light and went down to meet her son.

Outside, the sun was dipping low. The Canada geese were lifting in slow, deliberate arcs over the creek, honking in that ancient, orderly chorus as they crossed the sky. Tatiana paused on the porch for a breath of the cool autumn air, then followed her son into the gathering night

Chapter 4
Hunter's Moon

The Instagram story sequence hit like a slap of too much perfume in a windowless room—loud, saccharine, and suffocating.

Brittany Omen's face filled the screen first, lit by a ring light too bright for the hour. Her makeup was pristine in a way that suggested hours, not minutes: thick foundation laid like armor, lashes so long they cast shadows, lips swollen and glossed to a blinding pink. "Glam time with your fave blonde bombshell 💋✨," the caption cooed, accompanied by sparkles and a cherry emoji.

The next slide: a filtered close-up of her contouring palette, perfectly arranged, tagged with #BossBabeBeauty and #BanquetBaddie. Her voice, chirpy and robotic, narrated over sped-up footage of foundation blending—"Tonight's look is killer glam!"

In the background, slightly out of focus but still unmistakably present, was Ted Omen. Much older, much stiffer, his face stretched into a smile that didn't touch his eyes. His suit was over-pressed, his spray tan too orange under the LED lights, and he raised a glass of something amber with the stiff cheer of a man who knew his part but not the plot. Brittany didn't acknowledge him except to lean briefly toward him in one clip and kiss the air near his cheek.

Swipe up.

Now she was in a low-cut, skin-tight gown the color of champagne and just as subtle. Her surgically buoyant breasts were a focal point, framed like merchandise, while her voice purred, "Glam squad did it again!! Just a casual Thursday slay with my King 👑🤴 #PowerCouple #FallsminderFundraiser." Behind her, Ted lingered in the doorway like an accessory—smiling too wide, blinking too often, nodding as if someone had told him that's what supportive husbands do.

Final post: a Boomerang. Brittany twirling, dress shimmering, lips pursed in a kiss at the camera. In the mirror behind her, Ted adjusted his tie with mechanical care. His eyes, for a moment, weren't on her at all. They were somewhere else. Somewhere tired.

Group Chat – Good Omens

(Private, encrypted – because some comments should never leak to Page Six)

Freya (20, Brown): Brittany's latest Insta saga just dropped. I can feel the botox fumes through my phone. She's not being low key at all about attending Mom's work gala.

Ariadne (20, Columbia): Same. I've seen mannequins with more authentic facial expressions. #PlastiqueFantastique

Wolfgang (17, still at Lisgar): Please advise: At what point does a contour line become topographical? Asking for science.

Erinye (20, Yale): When the highlight has its own postal code, little brother. Also—did she really caption it "killer glam, literally"? Oof.

Freya: Subtle. Cringe.

Ariadne: Toxic like a spider bite.

Wolfgang: Incorrect. Necrotic spread is quite visible. Unlike Brittany's original skin tone.

Erinye: 💀 1 – Brittany's melanin: 0.

Freya: Did anyone else catch the hashtag *#BanquetBaddie*? Girl, the only thing she's serving is second-hand embarrassment.

Ariadne: And gluteal implants. Don't forget the gluteal implants.

Wolfgang: Statistically, the silicone volume present in that dress could plug the Rideau Canal leaks. Environmental stewardship?

Erinye: Sustainable queen! Reduce, reuse, recycle—resculpt.

Freya: Rebrand. She's one contour away from joining Ottawa's Gothic Revival architecture. All spires, no substance.

Ariadne: Dad—*sorry, The Unmentioned*—was lurking in the back like a malfunctioning animatronic. But Brittany didn't even tag him. Legendary.

Wolfgang: Perhaps he failed brand-guideline compliance. Wrong Pantone.

Erinye: Wolfie, you're savage tonight.

Wolfgang: Science is neutral. Shade is empirical.

Freya: Screenshotting that for merch. "Shade is Empirical."

Ariadne: Marketing minor strikes again.

Erinye: Anyway, shall we place bets on how many filters she stacked? I counted five—Paris, Oslo, Bali, Vivid Warm, and whatever that new "Porcelain Doll" update is.

Wolfgang: Filter count irrelevant. Underlying data corrupt.

Freya: Translation: she's catfishing the entire gala.

Ariadne: Speaking of fish, did you hear her say "just a casual Thursday slay"? Slay who, Brit? Grammar?

Erinye: Definitely syntax. RIP.

Wolfgang: Unrelated: Archival footage shows 100% correlation between overuse of "slay" and impending public relations disasters.

Freya: Foreshadowing noted, detective.

Ariadne: Okay, team. Symposiums await. Let's reconvene post-banquet. Keep your phones on. Something tells me tonight's plot twist won't need a filter.

Erinye: Roger that. May the ring lights dim and the Wi-Fi falter. I'd be happy if she just tripped.

Wolfgang: Logging off to recalibrate snark levels. Good luck, sisters.

Chat ended – 18:42

Outside, in the cool, windy evening, rising against early evening darkness of the October sky, the round, full Hunter's Moon rose low and heavy over Ottawa. Ottawa, Canada's quiet and picturesque capital, is a city of ordered charm. Unlike the bold energy of Toronto or the moody romance of Montreal, Ottawa moves with a bureaucratic hum—clean, serene, and slightly drowsy in its civility. The Rideau Canal, its waters glassy and obedient, slices neatly through the city, mirroring its reserved temperament. Ornate bridges, tidy parks, and the sharp silhouettes of federal buildings give Ottawa its uniquely polished face—beautiful, if a little banal. Bureaucrats abound. Like worker ants, in their brown and grey primness sacrificed long ago a fulfilling career for personal comfort, they have not necessarily having given up self-importance with their fuzzy hair and dress down under state demeanour. They have amongst them on an array of hobbies that rivals the hobby pursuits of any city anywhere. Ottawa, in consequence, is a banally pleasant city filled with clubs and Trivia nights and joggers, and a rush hour that starts at 3 pm.

The Museum of Nature, once a Victorian-era castle, rises from this calm like a carved memory. Its turrets and towers give the illusion of grandeur, while inside, the old limestone bones of the building whisper of centuries past. Converted from a castle to a museum, it retains a sense of haunted elegance—a perfect setting for natural curiosities, and unnatural events.

The amber light of the moon cast a wild, primal glow over the turrets of the Museum of Nature. Inside the stone tower, suspended from a wire above the atrium, hung a plastic replica of the moon—perfect in proportion, cold in texture, a manufactured echo of the ancient body outside. While it was a charming imitation, what the real moon offered in mystery and ancient power, the museum's facsimile mimicked in precision and sterility.

Tatiana thought the doubling of the plastic moon with the real one was an apt metaphor for the evening's gathering, and for Brittany Omen herself. Brittany—blonde, glossy, perpetually posed—gripped her husband's arm with a manicured hand, her teeth gleaming through a performative smile. She was the second Mrs. Omen, and to the untrained eye, she bore an eerie resemblance to the first: tall, elegant, camera-ready. But like the plastic moon above, she was a curated version. Where Tatiana had been wild and luminous, maybe even a bit much, Brittany was trim, waxed, botoxed, polished and calculated. Her silve gown was simple. She knew how to capture the light, not create it.

Tatiana Goode-Omen watched her from across the exhibit floor, her round face unreadable. Her satin coat was dusted with leaves from the museum courtyard, and there were a few stray dog hairs on it from her golden retriever named Ghost. Her dark curls were still tousled from the wind outside. She didn't try to tame them. She'd long ago given up performing for rooms like this. Even so, she turned heads with her energetic step and the move of her hips. As she jokingly pulled her teenage son forward into the room, her disarming laugh echoed through the marble hallway, and her smile flashed, still infectiously warm after all these years.

The museum's Insects of the World exhibit loomed around them: glass cases housing exotic, glistening beetles, hornets preserved mid-strike, spiders with venom sacs bulging like secrets. The artificial lighting above made their shadows dance. It was a carnival of danger locked behind glass.

Tatiana's breath caught as a dull ache pinched her chest—her heart reminding her, as it often did these days, that it had been through too much. Four pregnancies, including the high-risk triplets and her last child, Wolfgang, had left a toll that no one could see from the outside. A cardiologist might call it latent post-eclamptic damage. Tatiana called it a slow-motion reckoning.

She watched Brittany smooth down the sleeve of Ted Omen's jacket, adjusting his appearance like a curator tending to a wax figure. Brittany didn't love Ted—Tatiana knew that. She loved the proximity to power, the optics of marriage to a city councillor turned celebrity conservative pundit. Ted, for his part, loved being adored by women who reminded him of his prime.

But it was Tatiana who had walked beside the younger version of him when he was broke and furious, when he was less comical, less contrived and more authentic, railing against environmentalists while hiding overdue bills in the glovebox. It was Tatiana who had borne the weight—literal and emotional—of carrying his legacy. The triplets. Wolfgang. The family name. She felt it now, pressing against her ribcage like the phantom pressure of old bruises.

Ted Omen himself stood center-stage in his usual bluster: spray-tanned, broad-shouldered, propped up by a double-breasted suit that bulked where his body was, underneath, gaunt and twink-like. He grumbled about "eco-loonies" and "grant grifters" as he circulated among the donors and media flacks. The scent of old cologne clung to him, as thick as the entitlement in his voice.

On the edge of the gathering, Wolfgang Omen lingered near the shadowed side of a display case. Seventeen, tall, and handsome, with his mother's eyes and father's gait,, he was already absorbing the scene with forensic detachment. His phone was in his pocket, but his eyes never left the insects. He was especially drawn to a preserved warrior wasp, encased mid-flight, its abdomen frozen in the arc of a fatal sting. To Wolfgang, everything was data.

Tatiana felt him watching the world the way a predator watches a colony—quiet, cold, waiting for the system to show its weakness.

Cameras flashed as Brittany posed by the display on mimicry and deception—an exhibit that showcased prey insects who disguised themselves as predators. Tatiana allowed herself to laugh out loud, and she snapped a discrete photo with her iphone, to be shared later with her friends. The symbolism was too on the nose to ignore. Tatiana appreciated once again, as she had since her divorce, that if life took dramatically stupid turns, at least they generally turned out to be funny.

As the room buzzed with curated laughter and brittle champagne flutes, a single flash caught the glint of a glass case in the corner. It shimmered for a moment, casting twin shadows—one human, one plastic. No one noticed the movement behind the case. No one noticed the thin red petal that drifted from somewhere it did not belong.

Tatiana turned toward the staircase, her chest tight, her expression unreadable.

The night was just beginning.

Chapter 5
The Last Speech

The banquet hall at the Museum of Nature had been dressed in its finest deceit. Under the arched stone ceilings of what had once been a grand reading room—its bones still etched with the gravitas of early Canadian ambition—rows of linen-draped tables glittered with glassware and moral ambiguity. Candles flickered in ornate votives shaped like insects and leaves, casting long shadows across programs embossed with the evening's purpose: Fallsminder: A Gala for the Future. The irony hung thicker than the scent of garlic in the heirloom tomato hors d'oeuvres.

Partygoers in jewel-toned dresses floated between centerpieces of reclaimed wood and wildflowers, their laughter brittle and too bright. Politicos in tailored navy suits formed tight knots, exchanging guarded smiles and calculated glances over locally sourced wine. Every handshake was a strategy, every toast a performance. The Minister of Natural Resources posed beneath the skeleton of a hadrosaur, his smile tight, eyes scanning for cameras. And there were cameras. TV crews nestled discreetly behind potted ferns, their red lights blinking like the compound eyes of watchful insects. Radio hosts murmured into branded microphones, parsing platitudes for scandal. Columnists from The Hill Times leaned against the walls with notebooks half-filled and expressions half-amused.

Just beyond the velvet ropes, staff circulated with trays of canapés and warnings not to touch the exhibits. The Insects of the World gallery loomed at the edge of the hall, its glass cases glinting under museum lighting, artifacts from a quieter, more honest savagery.

Everyone in the room believed they knew what tonight was about: fundraising, alliances, appearances. But beneath the hum of cocktail chatter and clinking glasses, something darker stirred.

A whisper in the marble, perhaps, or a shadow behind the velvet curtain. Something had come in with the guests.

And it wasn't leaving.

"And now," said Marieve Dumont said into the microphone at the podium in front of the banquet hall, her silver hair glinting with her sequined silver dress, "I am pleased to introduce our legal counsel, Tatiana Goode-Omen, who will speak about our environmental conservation work."

Applause echoed through the banquet hall and Tatiana strode to the podium. She ran a hand through her long dark hair, pushing it back over her shoulders. She adjusted her glasses, then spoke: "Good evening and thank you—each and every one of you—for being here tonight. Your presence is not just appreciated; it is profoundly meaningful. This evening is more than a banquet. It is an affirmation of our shared stewardship—a collective vow to protect what is most elemental and most endangered: the living world.

Law, in its human form, can draft charters and render decisions. Law can also exculpate us, permit us, allow us to avoid our commitment to nature. We can contract out; the history of industrialization and law is one that largely fails to protect or even consider the natural environment. But there is a more ancient law—older than scroll or statute—the law of the Earth. This law does not ask for our authority; it asks for our respect. It does not compel obedience; it requires commitment.

The poet Mary Oliver once asked, "What is it you plan to do with your one wild and precious life?" Tonight, I ask: What will we do with our shared and sacred responsibility to this wild and precious Earth?

As we gather under this full moon, the hunter's moon, signifying the fullness of nature's harvest season, and raise our glasses, let us not forget the canopy of trees that breathes for us, the oceans that cradle life unseen, the soil that remembers every seed we sow. These are not resources. They are relationships. And our role is not to conquer them—but to care for them.

To be a steward is to act not just for today, but for generations yet unnamed. It is to answer the call of conscience with more than concern— with commitment. A commitment that begins here, in this room, and extends far beyond it.

The law may define our duties. But poetry reminds us of our purpose. And both lead us to this truth: that we belong to the Earth, not the other way around. Thank you for your generosity, your vision, and most of all, your commitment. Let this evening be not only a celebration, but a renewed promise—a promise to protect, to preserve, and to pass on this world in all its wonder.

"Thank you."

Tatiana sat down. The rumble of conversation and clinking of glasses and silverware began again.

Suddenly, Ted Omen stood at the front of the great hall. "Well, well," he said, the cavernous dome above echoing his voice with a faint, hollow resonance. Ted had not been on the evening's program, but, typically of a politician, he had muscled his way to the podium. His tall, lean frame cast a shadow on the banner, obscuring the words, "Environmental Conservation Fundraiser." The lighting from the Insects of the World exhibit gave his face a strange hue, one moment green, the next golden, flickering with shadows of the beetles and wasps suspended behind him.

He cleared his throat dramatically, paused for effect while scanning the room, and at last launched into his speech: "Ladies and gentlemen," he began, voice rich with condescension, "thank you for joining us tonight in this cathedral of science and hysteria." There were polite chuckles. "I've always said, if you give a bug a good press agent, someone will find a way to ban it." Ted then waved a handkerchief in his right hand, winked, and made it disappear. There was a smattering of applause, and were a few groans, in response to his sleight of hand.

Ted went on: "Oh indeed, thank you for coming tonight to this magnificent palace of natural science, a place where bugs are preserved more carefully than common sense. I stand before you not as an enemy of the environment, but as a loyal friend to reason—an endangered species, it seems, in these so-called enlightened times.

"Unfortunately," he went on, "Your efforts are misplaced, misguided, even foolhardy. We are told, relentlessly, that the Earth is dying. Melting. Drowning. Burning.

As if our home planet were a poorly maintained Airbnb. But ask yourselves: if climate change were real, would it not have already canceled spring by now? I see tulips every May. Do we not have a thriving tulip festival? Of course we do. Case closed.

Now, they say we must "decarbonize." But consider this: humans are carbon-based lifeforms. Ergo, if we eliminate carbon, we eliminate ourselves. This is not environmentalism—it's existential nihilism in a compostable wrapper. We used to say "reduce, reuse, recycle" but that lacks vision. Innovate! Move on! This planet outlives its usefulness? We find another!! We must ever move forward!"

Let us also talk about "green energy." Wind turbines kill birds. Solar panels block the sun from reaching the grass. Are we really saving the planet by blinding our lawns and terrorizing the geese? I think not.

I recently read that cows produce methane. But so do humans. So if we're serious about emissions, perhaps we should regulate burritos before we ban beef. Just a thought.

They want us to "consume less." But I ask: how do we grow the economy without shopping? If buying a plastic garden flamingo on Amazon destroys the rainforest, then frankly, the rainforest may have overreacted.

Let me leave you with this. Trees? Overrated. They've had a monopoly on oxygen production for millennia. It's time to diversify. If we must go to Mars to re-settle, if we must re-make our world, then go we must.

Thank you."

Tatiana, wearing her nametag that said, Legal Counsel, Environmental Conservation, stood near the back of the room, her posture elegant, her eyes cold. She held her glass of white wine loosely, as if it were simply a prop. Her heart fluttered uncomfortably in her chest; the pain dull but insistent. Her thoughts drifted between the past, the handsome young man she had married, and the grotesque caricature of him presently in front of her, recklessly and boldly contradicting the point of the evening's fundraiser, and her life's work. She fantasized about him collapsing behind the podium. Every divorce is a kind of murder. Tatiana had given up on his dream; perhaps that's where it began. Perhaps, she sighed, when she was overwhelmed by care for the children, when she did not actively support his recycling initiatives, she killed the relationship. Love, after all, is not a feeling. It's a decision and a practice. It's a choice.

Despite the darkness of these thoughts, it was very hard for Tatiana not to laugh. But then she glanced at her son and felt simply sad. Her son could see right through the ridiculousness of the speech, she could tell, and his cheeks were flushed with embarrassment.

Closer to the stage, Marieve Dumont clenched her jaw. The environmental fundraiser's eyes blazed as Ted railed against "tree-huggers," "eco-hysterics," and "climate scammers." Nearby, Max Springhill, the sharp-suited tech investor, took mental notes—calculating not the truth of Ted's words but the public reaction to them. Marieve Dumont leaned towards Max and said, softly, and sarcastically: "it would be a real shame if something terrible happened to Ted Omen."

Brittany Omen, all bonded teeth and vacant, glassy eyes under her faux lashes, twirled her hair extension around in a manicured finger, and stepped away from her husband's spotlight. Her expression slipped, a flicker of something dark passing through her perfect façade. "I need the restroom," she murmured to no one in particular, heels clicking as she vanished down the corridor.

Ted swatted at an invisible fly and grumbled something about needing a real drink. Then, puffing his chest out, he strode toward the upper floors, his voice fading but his shadow long and imposing.

Tatiana watched him go, her fingers tightening around the stem of her glass. She didn't follow. Not yet.

In the hush that followed his departure, the exhibit returned to its soft, buzzing ambiance. Cameras clicked again. Max leaned over to whisper something into Marieve's ear, but she ignored him.

Somewhere upstairs, a glass case clicked shut. Somewhere out of sight, a sealed airlock hissed softly. A change in the air—barely perceptible, but real. And below, the gathered guests carried on sipping their drinks, unaware that the night had just turned fatal.

Chapter 6
Death in the Dark

The museum's third floor was dimly lit, and shadowy, with moonlight flowing in through its large windows onto the white marble floors, its light doubled by the electric light emanating from the plastic moon decoration hanging from the ceiling, Ambient light from the exhibit displays casting shifting insectile shadows along the tiled floor. Downstairs, most fundraiser guests had trickled out, their laughter and murmurs echoing faintly down the stairwells.

In the quiet dark of night, the upstairs halls of Ottawa's Museum of Nature had felt less like a museum and more like the abandoned corridors of a forgotten palace—one where the air had been thick with memory and glass.

Gone had been the daytime bustle, the laughter of children and the soft murmur of docents. In its place: silence, deep and velvety, so complete it had hummed in the ears. The chandeliers above, normally brilliant with light, had loomed as dark, skeletal cages, their crystals catching the faintest glimmer of moonlight that had slipped between the heavy stone and stained glass.

The marble floors had stretched out in long, cold lanes, polished to the point that they reflected the world above them like water. At night, those reflections had rippled with shadow. A lone red exit sign had thrown a distant crimson glow against the far wall—enough to cast long, creeping silhouettes behind the velvet rope barriers and glass display cases.

The exhibits had been asleep, but not dormant. Taxidermied owls had stared with uncanny awareness, their glass eyes catching stray light with a glint that had felt too knowing. The insects, frozen in eternal crawl, had seemed poised to move, their antennae angled like they were listening for something that stirred only after hours.

The carved archways and pointed windows of the upper galleries had become gothic and grand in the absence of light, their angles more pronounced, their purpose more mysterious.

The halls had felt longer, the ceilings higher. Footsteps—if any were made—had echoed too loudly. Every creak of wood or distant settling of stone had sounded like a whisper, or a warning.

Even the air had felt older at night in the museum—slightly cooler, tinged with dust and something else, something harder to name. The weight of centuries. The smell of pressed velvet and old paper and limestone bones. It had been a place that remembered.

And for those who had stood there long enough, very still, it had become clear that they were the exhibit, not the observer. Because in the upstairs halls of the Museum of Nature, after dark, the past had watched them

The air was still, too still.

At precisely 9:00 p.m., first a gargle, then a sharp, startled cry tore through the quiet.

The echoing sound of running footsteps followed. Security guards, startled into motion, charged toward the source of the scream. The door to the third-floor bathroom stood slightly ajar, a dark smudge on its edge.

Inside, on the marble tile of the corridor alongside the stairwell, the outstretched frame of Ted Omen lay sprawled on the cold, speckled tiles, crumpled like a two-dimensional piece of paper. His dark hair was askew around his head, with grey roots now showing as a halo around his head. His mouth was slack, with drool trickling down to his chin, cakey and orange, revealing foundation and concealer. Where the makeup was smudged, there was a faint trace of freckles across his cheeks. One of his shoes had fallen off, making very noticeable the height-enhancing lift it contained. Omen's eyes were wide and glassy. As he lay on the ground on his back, one hand was curled awkwardly beneath him; the other was outstretched, as if he had tried to ward off something unseen.

With the police station just around the corner, police and Paramedics arrived within minutes, but it was too late. The lead medic paused, frowning at the odd coloration creeping up Ted's arm and the small, jagged marks on the heel of his palm. Bite marks? He glanced at the museum curator who had followed them in and said, "Call the Coroner."

The hush around the scene was broken only by murmurs of staff and uniformed voices on radios. Guests were held at the exits as a precaution. Word spread quickly, first in whispers throughout the building, then on social media — a man was dead. Ted Omen was dead.

Wolfgang Omen stood just beyond the crowd's edge, silent, still. His pale blue eyes did not leave the sight of his father's body. Tatiana, beside him, started shaking and reached to touch his shoulder. Wolfgang pulled away. His face was blank, in that moment resembling the frozen mask that was his father's. But inside, his mind ticked like a metronome, counting: fang length, venom delivery method, latency. He mentally eliminated snakes — unlikely. Scorpions — not precise enough. A spider, maybe. Something small. Intelligent. Deliberate.

Tatiana had to sit down. She collapsed heavily onto a bench beside the corridor, and, she started to cry. Lying there, Ted had looked so vulnerable. Memories of his youthful grin, of his face when he held their children, of him opening the door to their first house, flashed into her mind. It had been a long time since she had thought of him that way, vulnerable, human. Seeing him dead like that made her think for the first time in years that he did not deserve to die. She wished now he could have had forty more years of mediocrity.

Standing above her, in her glittering gown, Brittany was weeping loudly.

In Wolfgang's pocket, his phone buzzed. A message from one of his sisters:

"I saw the news on Twitter. Is it true? Is Dad the dead body at the museum?", messaged Freya, from her Yale email address.

Wolfgang replied, "there is no good way to say it. Yes, Dad is dead."

There was a pause.

"That's awful. That's an awful way to go," wrote Freya.

"Yes, very sad. I am so sad now." Wrote Erinye.

"Awful," chimed in Ariadne.

"I guess we need to go home," wrote Freya. The other girls swiftly "liked" the message.

"Let's all look at flights."

There was a long pause. Wolfgang could feel his heart in his chest as he stood in the museum corridor. And then, another message, in reply, "Did mom finally kill him?" It was Ariadne, the middle sister, writing from Princeton.

"No. Mom didn't kill him. She didn't need to. He killed her slowly, remember? All those pregnancies. The preeclampsia. Her heart. He's the Black Widower," this message was from Erinye, the youngest of the triplets, by fifteen minutes, writing from Harvard.

"I wonder who killed him. I mean, who *didn't* want to at some point," wrote Ariadne. "Brittany," wrote Freya, "She was happy with him. So it would not have been Brittany."

Wolfgang didn't reply. He put his phone back into his pocked. He turned back to the bathroom. There, on the floor just beside the baseboard, unnoticed by the medics, was a faint trail of puncture-shaped drops — not blood, but something darker. Something venomous. His breath shallow, Wolfgang stepped back, letting the uniformed bodies swirl in. He watched the drama unfold with the careful detachment of a scientist observing a specimen under glass.

Outside the bathroom, the museum's Victorian shadows closed in tighter. Somewhere, beneath glass or behind stone, something had been set loose.

Chapter 7
The Web Tightens

The laughter had stopped.

What was left in the banquet hall at the Museum of Nature was the sound of high heels pacing stone floors, champagne flutes trembling just slightly in manicured hands, and the quiet, unmistakable thrum of fear beginning to curdle in the air.

The party had ended without a toast. A scream—sharp, human, unplaceable—had slashed through the chatter like a scalpel through silk. And then: silence, except for the hurried stamp of security boots and the sudden stutter of someone's dropped phone recording nothing at all.

Now, no one was allowed to leave.

The doors had been quietly, efficiently locked. Two uniformed officers stood by the exits, eyes flat. A third barked into a radio that sputtered and hissed like a cornered snake. Word had spread fast—someone was dead. Someone important. Possibly murdered.

The guests lingered in uneasy clusters, eyes darting toward the museum's tall windows, where rain streaked like claw marks against the glass. The chandeliers above seemed too bright now, too surgical, exposing the nerves beneath the party's polished skin. A woman in emerald silk whispered to her husband through clenched teeth. A junior aide to a cabinet minister fidgeted with his cufflink until it snapped. Even the servers stood still, their trays long forgotten.

Some drifted toward the insect exhibit, drawn like moths to the quiet hum of the darkness beyond the barricade. The glass cases—so pristine before—now loomed like coffins. No one spoke of the broken display, the shards that had once held something venomous and very much alive. Not out loud.

And then the waiting began in earnest.

Thirty minutes. Forty-five. An hour.

The tension thickened like fog. The museum, already ancient in its bones, seemed to inhale the unease, stone walls flexing with old secrets. What had started as a fundraiser now felt like a trap. One of them had done it. Or one of them was next.

And outside, unseen but inevitable, the detectives were coming.

At last, after precisely one hour, Detective Clark St. John stepped into the third-floor corridor of the Museum of Nature, his boots clicking sharply, and sliding a bit against the marble. The RCMP officer's dark silhouette cut a lean line through the gathering chaos. Tall, gaunt, he walked with a slight limp. He wore a rumpled trench coat. The lingering scent of faint cologne from the evenings' partygoers didn't mask the metallic sting of death in the air.

"Who found the body?" he asked crisply, snapping on a pair of gloves.

One of the uniformed security guards pointed toward the museum's night manager, a pale woman in her thirties who looked as though she'd aged a decade in the past hour. "He was... just there," she murmured. "Like he fell. Or was dropped."

St. John crouched beside the corpse. The faint swelling on the palm, now more pronounced, held his gaze. Too localized for an allergic reaction. Too intentional for coincidence. He scanned the floor. Something glistened near the baseboard — not blood. Resinous. Dark. The kind of thing that would dry into a crust the colour of molasses. A venom trail.

"Cord this section off. I want full forensics sweep of the gallery too. Including the insect exhibits."

"Sir?" the officer nearest him raised a brow.

"There's no way this was natural. Something — or someone — set this in motion."

Downstairs, the guests were held in tense limbo. The once-bubbly champagne event had curdled into hushed panic. Tatiana sat on a bench beside the second-floor atrium, her fingers twisting the silver bracelet on her wrist. Her pulse hadn't slowed. She hadn't touched her wine glass since the scream. She wasn't crying anymore.

Across from her, Marieve Dumont paced like a jaguar in a cage. "I'm not sorry he's dead," she whispered. "He tried to gut our entire conservation campaign on live TV. But…not like this. Not tonight. This'll be all over the press."

Tatiana looked up; her voice quiet. "He was still the father of my children."

Marieve's gaze softened, then flared with curiosity. "Do you think… was it an accident? A real insect? Something escaped?"

Tatiana didn't answer. Her mind was elsewhere — in a sterile birthing room years ago, monitors screaming as her heart faltered and the physicans rushed her into an anteroom for an emergency C-section. They had loved natural life so much back then, she and Ted, that they had done no ultrasounds: they had not known she was carrying triplets. And then in a courtroom. And then in a dimly lit bedroom when Ted had stopped touching her. She remembered it all too clearly.

By the glass doors leading to the inner courtyard, Brittany Omen dabbed her eyes with a crumpled linen handkerchief, mascara bleeding into the creases beneath her Botox-frozen eyes. She had reappeared after "getting air", although Tatiana and Wolfgang had heard Brittany talking to her publicist. Her voice, though tearful, was clear. Polished.

A junior officer approached. "We need to speak with all immediate family. And spouses. Can you come with me, ma'am?"

"I'm his widow," Brittany sniffled. "Of course."

"I should come too," said Tatiana, touching Wolfgang on the arm, "I am the mother of his children, his *ex*-widow I suppose."

Behind a museum bench on the third floor, barely shielded by shadows, something gleamed in the low light — a small, velvet-lined case, half-tucked into a vent grille. It would remain unseen, for now. A vital clue nestled in silence.

Downstairs, Max Springhill's phone buzzed again. "No, we are *not* issuing a statement yet," he hissed to his assistant. "Wait until we know cause of death. If this was foul play, we pivot to security failures. If not — we mourn. Quietly. With hashtags."

He ended the call, rubbing his temple, then glanced toward Tatiana. Her calm unnerved him. She was watching everything. Springhill thought for a moment that, although no one he knew liked Ted, Tatiana liked him least of all.

Detective St. John returned downstairs, face unreadable. He asked for Tatiana, Brittany, and Wolfgang to join him in the director's office.

Wolfgang had already moved. He stood beside the insect exhibit, staring through the glass. A Brazilian wandering spider — dead, taxidermied — preserved in aggressive posture.

"What are you thinking?" Tatiana whispered as they passed, " are you ok?"

"I'm thinking," Wolfgang said quietly, "someone used the museum's theme as a weapon."

Upstairs, unnoticed by all, the venom trail dried to a crisp. The Victorian shadows of the museum stretched longer with nightfall, cloaking secrets in architecture designed to awe. Somewhere in the echoing silence, a predator had shed its skin.

Chapter 8
On the Scent

Detective Clark St. John stood just inside the glass vestibule of the Museum of Nature, collar damp, the shoulders of his tan overcoat creased from the long night. The museum, largely emptied now of its posturing donors and faux-earnest influencers, felt like a cathedral of bones—marble floors glistening faintly in the overhead security light, shadows casting long, accusatory shapes against the fossilized remains of former kingdoms.

He watched the janitor's mop bucket slosh around a streak of muddy footprints—someone had run just before the scream. Someone always runs.

He found Marieve Dumont in a side room stacked with informational banners and the corpse of a half-dismantled pop-up display about pollinators. She was sitting on a packing crate, her long scarf coiled like a strangler fig at her feet. She looked up at him like a hawk disturbed at its nest.

"Since you asked me to wait to speak with you, I suppose you think I did it," she said. Her voice was edged in fatigue and unspent rage.

"I think perhaps you wanted to," St. John said, leaning on the doorframe. "That's often enough."

"I hated him," she said. "That's not a secret. But hating someone doesn't mean you kill them."

"No," he said. "But it might mean you don't mind if someone else does. Or you might help them do it."

She didn't flinch. "Poetic justice," she murmured. "Ted Omen was poison, Detective. All I ever did was try to counteract the venom he spilled into public policy."

St. John glanced at her hands—clean, no polish, and he noticed the thick scent of her perfume, Chanel No. 5, elegant, classic, old but never out of fashion. Still, the eyes. Eyes like firelight on broken glass.

"I heard you argued with him. At the gala."

"I told him that this was an environmental fundraiser, and chastised him for derailing it," she said. "He told me to smile more and asked if I was on my period."

St. John jotted something in his notebook. Not because he needed it, but because silence was more revealing when you broke it with a pen.

"You can go," Detective Clark St. John said to her, "but don't leave town."

Further down the corridor, St. John found Max Springhill pacing like a caged civet in the loading bay, phone in one hand, panic barely reined in.

"You don't pace like a man shocked by murder," St. John said. "You pace like a man who just lost his investment."

Springhill blinked. His face was the kind that had been coached to look sincere by three different PR firms and still hadn't quite nailed it.

"Look," he said. "I'm not heartbroken Ted's dead. But I didn't kill him. I didn't need to."

"Because you were on the verge of a major tech rollout with him," St. John said. "Environmental monitoring apps for extractive industries. Greenwashed profit."

Springhill frowned. "It was supposed to help the planet."

"Sure," St. John said. "Sounded like Ted was very interested in that type of social enterprise. Same way a leash helps a dog run free."

He watched Max squirm. The man had clean shoes, but there was a smear of lipstick near his collarbone—subtle, expensive, and not his. He also smelled familiar, Clark St. John realized with a smile, noting the scent of Chanel No. 5.

Alone again, St. John stepped out into the courtyard where the fountain had long since been drained for winter. Rain pattered across the dry stone like Morse code tapping from the grave.

He lit a cigarette. He shouldn't. His lungs hated it and his doctor hated it more. But it helped him think. He thought about how men like Ted always surrounded themselves with youth and gloss and surface. Brittany. The plastic moonlight of a second wife. Brittany was perhaps fortunate; youth is a non-renewable resource, and as she aged she and would never have lasted long in Ted's world. But someone like Tatiana… She had the kind of intelligence that didn't require sequins. A woman who had lived, not posed. A woman with a law degree, a medical history written in pain, and four children she'd raised like saplings in a storm. Clearly Springhill understood the value of a mature woman's company.

Clark St. John, contemplating the fact that he was now hungry for breakfast, realized, with a kind of melancholy clarity, that he'd like to have dinner with someone like her. Maybe talk about the law and its failings. Maybe Tatiana would ask him questions, which would be a relief for him, not to be investigating but for someone to know him. He would like not to look just at beauty. Not to talk politics. Just to spend some time telling the truth.

But he had a case to solve.

Chapter 9

Hidden Venom

The night outside in Ottawa was sharp with October's breath and slicked in silver by the full Hunter's Moon. That moon hung low and bloated in the sky, its pale light bruising the city in unnatural hues—neither warm nor cold, but something older, something watchful.

Maple leaves, once blazing with autumn's fire, now curled black on their edges, fluttered down like burnt paper from the boughs above. They scraped the pavement softly as they fell, a thousand little whispers no one stopped to hear. The wind carried them through alleyways and across the Canal's stone banks, dragging them in restless circles as though stirred by something more than weather.

Clouds were beginning to gather above the Parliament buildings, thin at first—streaks like torn gauze across the stars—but thickening fast, coiling around the moon's glow like fingers around a throat. The light dimmed, subtly at first, then with purpose. The kind of darkness that doesn't fall, but rises.

Along Wellington Street, lamplight cast distorted reflections on wet pavement, stretching shadows into strange angles. The Gothic silhouettes of the Peace Tower and the East Block loomed darker than the sky, stone monuments that remembered things they were never meant to tell.

At the far end of the city core, the Canadian Museum of Nature stood still and heavy, its turrets and gargoyles watching the streets with glassy indifference. Inside, its exhibits slept under lock and key—but outside, the city shifted. Something unseen had changed. The air no longer merely chilled; it pressed in, expectant.

And somewhere, beneath the hiss of tires on wet asphalt, between the dry rustle of dying leaves and the soft thud of falling acorns, there was the unmistakable silence of something waiting to happen.

Ottawa was wrapped in its rituals of diplomacy and denial, but the night knew better. The moon was full. The leaves were falling.

And something was coming undone.

The director's office on the second floor of the Museum of Nature had once been the private quarters of a curator in the early 20th century. Now, it bore the bland uniformity of institutional interiors—standard-issue chairs, a desktop computer blinking idly, a brittle orchid plant by the window.

Detective Clark St. John leaned against the edge of the desk, arms folded, as he surveyed the trio before him. Tatiana, upright, composed, her lawyer's instincts whirring beneath her calm gaze. Wolfgang, perched silently on a corner chair, his long fingers tapping his thigh in an uneven rhythm. Brittany, in a designer coat too thin for October, clutching a tissue like a prop, eyes swollen but dry.

"I'm going to ask each of you where you were when the scream was heard," St. John said, voice low but firm.

"I was near the atrium," Tatiana said. "With my son."

Wolfgang gave a curt nod.

"I stepped outside," Brittany offered. "To take a call. You can ask my assistant."

"We will," St. John said, not writing it down. "Anyone notice anything unusual about Ted's behaviour tonight?"

"He was odious, pompous, and smug, offending everyone with half a brain, directly contradicting what we are all working for," Tatiana replied. "But that was not unusual."

Wolfgang's face flushed, "I only saw him onstage," he said, "we had not talked in a while."

St. John looked at her intently for a long moment, then looked away. "Brittany," he said, looking over to her, "you spent more time with him, yes, getting ready and such? I saw some footage on social media. How was he acting?"

Brittany gasped at Tatiana, "Poor dear! I thought he looked sweaty," Brittany said. "And irritable. He said the lighting was bothering him."

"Lighting?" St. John repeated.

"From my selfie lights. He had sensitive eyes," Brittany said quickly.

St. John let the silence fill the room. "Did he have any allergies?"

"No," all three said at once.

"Curious," the detective said. "Because the coroner noted signs of anaphylaxis—or envenomation. And we found traces of venom on the doorframe leading into the washroom."

Brittany looked sharply at that. "Venom? From what?"

"We're still determining," he said, watching her closely. "It's not common. Not native."

Tatiana turned her head, voice steady. "You think someone brought something into the museum."

"I think," St. John replied, "that someone used the museum itself as a murder weapon."

"And," said Tatiana, "also as a stage, no?"

St. John raised an eyebrow. "Yes," he said, "yes this was quite theatrical. Performative, one might say."

In the exhibit hall, a museum technician named Rhonda Jenkins was quietly sweeping glass shards into a dustpan beneath a large "Predators of the Tropics" case. The spider case — usually holding a tarantula display — was cracked along one corner. It wasn't clear when the break had happened.

Behind her, a junior officer radioed in. "Yeah. Broken glass. Display compromised. Looks like someone accessed the case."

Rhonda frowned and bent lower. On the floor beneath the case lay a scatter of crushed pink rose petals, strangely out of place.

She stood and lifted a corner of the museum's guest brochure from the floor. The corner was slick with something — not water. It shimmered faintly in the light.

She sniffed. Sweet, cloying. Familiar.

"Perfume," she murmured. "Paris Hilton."

Detective St. John returned to the scene of the crime just after midnight, walking slowly down the corridor to the third-floor bathroom.

The museum was silent now, sealed and emptied of all but staff and police. His steps echoed in the hush.

He paused at the doorframe. Forensics had already collected samples, but he ran his gloved hand gently along the baseboard.

A faint smear remained, oily and dark.

From behind him came a voice: "It was intentional."

Wolfgang.

The boy had come back.

"You shouldn't be here," St. John said.

"I couldn't sleep," Wolfgang said. "And I think I can help."

St. John raised an eyebrow.

"I think the spider used was a Sicarius," Wolfgang continued. "Six-eyed sand spider. Buries itself in substrate. Has necrotic venom. It wouldn't kill fast, unless directly injected into a vein. But the signs—flesh discolouration, neural shock—they match."

"How would someone get one?" St. John asked.

"There are illegal breeders," Wolfgang said. "Collectors. Entomologists. Or someone who has... access."

"To a museum," St. John said slowly. " A public museum."

"To someone who asked questions," Wolfgang corrected. "Brittany. I saw her. She asked the entomologist about how long spiders live. If any of them were active."

St. John's lips thinned. "Why didn't you say that earlier?"

"Because I didn't want to believe it," Wolfgang said. "Because Brittany was listening. Because my mother doesn't need to hear it. Because Ted Omen was my father and I loved my father, despite all of it, despite everything. And because I don't know who Brittany really is. None of us do."

They stood in silence. The corridor was cold.

Then, St. John spoke, "Listen kid, I know it's been a rough night for you. And I am sorry about your dad. But Brittany seems like the one person who liked your father. On the other hand, there is a person who is quite intelligent, had advance access to the museum as an organizer of the event, and did not like the deceased one bit."

"Marieve Dumont was in the rooms below all evening," said Wolfgang, " She hated my father, but she is a social butterfly."

St. John reached over to Wolfgang and put his hand gently on the boy's shoulder. "Son, I wasn't thinking of Marieve Dumont. I was thinking of your mother."

Wolfgang drew away from him sharply, "My mother is not a killer." Brittany liked my father's *money*. Maybe he was between her and that payday," and the he said again, my mother is not a killer."

Behind them, the air was still thick with the scent of lilacs and rot.

Chapter 10

We Only Kill Those We Love

The Museum of Nature wore its silence like a veil, its once lively marble halls now echoing only the scrape of cautious footsteps and the low hum of after-hours cleaning crews. Detective Clark St. John stood beneath the great whale skeleton, arms folded, trench coat draped like an accusation. He watched the Honourable Andrew Jones-Middleton, Canada's Environment Minister, pace a polite distance from the ammonite exhibit, flanked loosely by a security aide.

The Minister looked out of place—not for his sharp grey suit or the polished confidence with which he carried himself, but for the vague unease that clung to him. He was used to press scrums and policy announcements, not murder inquiries.

"I understand you attended the gala," St. John said without preamble.

"Yes," the Minister replied, straightening. "The Fallsminder group invited me. It was a cause I thought worth supporting. Optically, it aligned well with the ministry's messaging on community-based environmental leadership."

"Optically," St. John repeated, deadpan.

Jones-Middleton stiffened. "Detective, are you implying something?"

St. John gestured toward the balcony where the murder had occurred. "Just clarifying the distinction between support and optics. Because it seems, short days before the murder, Councillor Omen gave a very confident interview about his AI casino project moving forward—approval expected soon from the federal Environment Minister. He had the kind of confidence of a man who has government on an undisclosed payroll."

The Minister blinked slowly, like a man processing the setup to a joke. "And?"

"And you're that Minister."

Jones-Middleton exhaled sharply, half a laugh, half a warning. "Let's not inflate Ted Omen's importance. He was a City Councillor and entrepreneur with probably one term left, and delusions of grandeur. I'm the Federal Environment Minister. The government of Canada is a national organization, you realize. I spend my days being screamed at by oil lobbyists and international trade representatives with billions of dollars at stake. You think I'd take a bribe from a man trying to build a slot machine emporium on the Rideau Falls?"

St. John didn't flinch. "I think a man's ambition has little to do with his capacity to corrupt or be corrupted. Sounds like we aren't talking about whether you would take a bribe, though, Minister. Seems like we are discussing the price."

Jones-Middleton's eyes narrowed. "Detective, I was with my staff during the entire time of the gala. We were downstairs. I gave a short speech, had a drink, shook hands, and left with the rest of my team. I assume you're verifying that."

"We are."

"Then unless you have surveillance footage of me brandishing a venomous spider, I suggest you direct your questions elsewhere."

St. John nodded, slowly. "Of course. Just one more thing, Minister— how often do billion-dollar oil companies thank you for your ethical scrutiny?"

Jones-Middleton smirked. "They don't. But they're still standing. That's the difference between resisting pressure and needing it."

The conversation ended with a handshake that was more ritual than rapport. The minister turned and walked back toward his aide, his steps a touch quicker than before.

As he moved to leave, the Honourable Minister turned back to St. John, " oh," he said, "and by the way, this whole thing was rather theatrical, did you notice? I would think you had been around the block enough times to notice that theatricality is not really the Canadian government's style. We don't really advertise. If I had done it," he winked, "you would not have such a good reason to suspect me. No," he said, "this sort of dramatic spectacle is how we kill the ones we love. Good day."

St. John remained beneath the bones of the whale, looking up at its bleached arch. In a city like Ottawa, you didn't always need the body to smell a cover-up. You just had to listen for who rushed to explain themselves first.

Chapter 12

The Sting

The rain hadn't stopped. It slicked the capital in a film of silence and silvery puddles, pooling in cobblestones, sluicing along the gutters, and giving everything—from the Parliament's green, gothic buttresses to the peaked roof of the Chateau Laurier hotel beside them, to gargoyles on the roof of the Museum of Nature - a pale, saturated sheen. The light had gone grey again. It was always grey this time of year.

Detective Clark St. John stood just outside the museum's east staff entrance, his trench coat soaked dark at the hem and collecting rain along its upturned collar. He didn't move much, didn't need to. He smoked without urgency, letting the cigarette's ember barely fight the damp. Beneath the coat, his pressed shirt had wilted at the collar, and a faint smudge of ink from last night's notes ghosted his hand. He looked, in every respect, like a man who hadn't slept and didn't expect to.

Inside, the museum buzzed again—but not with schoolchildren or tourists. Officers moved quietly now, voices low, avoiding the gaze of the insects in the display cases. The building had become something else: not a museum, but a hive. Controlled chaos. Predators and prey under the same stone roof.

Back in Centretown, the political staffers had been up before the daylight. The political staff at the Ministry of the Environment hadn't even gone to bed. Phones pinged through curated spreadsheets, damage assessments, and rapid response memos. A cabinet communications aide barked orders over speakerphone while someone else drafted preemptive tweets expressing "deep sorrow" and "respect for the ongoing investigation." An MP's assistant rehearsed his boss's alibi for the fourth time, voice low and tight, as if saying it often enough would make it truth.

None of this was unusual. In Ottawa, storylines were spun faster than the red maple leaves that blew, kicked up by the autumn winds. By 9 a.m., every political figure who had attended the fundraiser at the Museum of Nature the night before had a backdated calendar entry, a not-quite-factual quote ready for the press, and at least two versions of plausible deniability. The machine didn't stall for murder. It adjusted.

It was a city built on old lies, scaffolded with new ones, polished with press releases and sealed with smiles.

Detective St. John knew this. He'd once arrested a minister's son for assault at an embassy party. The charges disappeared before the ink dried. That was a long time ago. He still wore the trench coat from that night.

He flicked the cigarette into a puddle and stepped inside.

On the third floor, Brittany Omen sat alone in a bright interrogation room that didn't match the rest of the museum's gothic grandeur. A camera blinked red above her, capturing every breath. The vial sat on the metal table between them like an accusation.

St. John stepped in, coat dripping, eyes flat. He dropped a folder beside the vial.

"Your fingerprints are on the broken glass case," he said, without sitting.

Brittany blinked, mascara smudged in a way that might have been planned. "I was curious," she said. "That's not illegal."

"You asked a lot of questions about venom. About lifespan. About spiders that don't belong in this hemisphere."

"I'm an influencer," she smiled thinly. "We ask about a lot of things."

He didn't return the smile. "We spoke to the entomologist. He remembers you. Remembers your perfume. Paris Hilton. Sweet. Familiar."

She went still.

St. John continued, voice low. "You knew what the spider could do. You timed it. You let it loose in the one place your husband wouldn't be watched."

"Late husband," she said quickly.

"I guess that makes you a black widow," St. John mused.

" I guess," Brittany said, clicking her fingernails on her Gucci handbag, " you don't know what it's like to feel expendable, to be nobody, to be poor. To be unseen, I guess you don't even know." A solitary tear slid down Brittany's right cheek, "I am not saying I did it, Detective. I am just saying you don't know me."

Detective St. John raised his eyebrow, cleared his throat, and said, "lots of people are poor. Lots of people marry for money. Fewer, though, commit cold blooded murder."

Brittany laughed, "We do remember the ones who do."

The hallway outside the room was empty but for Wolfgang, who stood with a museum guard, watching through the observation glass. His face was unreadable, pale and fixed. One hand clutched his phone, where the group chat with his sisters still glowed.

"Mom didn't kill Dad," the latest message read. "But maybe Brittany did."

As officers prepared the warrant paperwork and news outlets readied their noon-hour segments, Ottawa continued to hum. Umbrellas bobbed like beetles across Sparks Street. Cars hissed along Wellington. And beneath the city's polished surface, something colder stirred.

Justice wasn't clean. It wasn't quick.

But today, at least, it was creeping closer.

And it wore a wet trench coat.

Chapter 13
Echoes in the Glasshouse

Canada's pleasant appearing, deeply quiet capital city wore its dusk like a crime it didn't regret. The October sky hung low over Ottawa like a false apology—clouded, soft-edged, and just polite enough to unsettle you. It was the kind of sky that didn't storm, just threatened to, the way a bureaucrat in a crisp suit might smile while quietly dismissing your tax appeal. Canadian weather, like Canadian manners, had a way of cloaking menace in courtesy. The clouds didn't roar. They murmured. They attended. They waited for you to make the first move. And just like the memo that ruins your life without a signature, that sky never broke—it just hovered, heavy and gray, pressing down like paperwork you didn't know was already filed against you.

October had pulled its grey coat tighter, and the streetlamps flickered like dying confessions. The air was cold and smelled faintly of rain, diesel, and something older—like mothballs and secrets. Ottawa, for all its polite teeth, was a town with skeletons stuffed into its stone walls, and tonight, they were rattling.

Detective Clark St. John lit a cigarette with a hand that didn't quite tremble. He'd been staring at the Museum of Nature from across the street, the way a man might eye a church he didn't believe in but couldn't quite ignore. Its turrets clawed at the sky. The windows glowed faintly from within. Some rooms still held warmth. Most didn't.

Inside, the last officers were packing up. Brittany Omen had been led away in a car with no sirens but plenty of silence. The kind that said you weren't going home again, not tonight. Maybe not ever. Her Instagram account was unusually inactive, maybe forever.

St. John stepped into the foyer, his trench coat shedding drops onto the stone floor like melting snow. The museum smelled of wax and limestone and the faint ghost of something venomous. He paused beneath the arch of the insect gallery, where glass cases stood in polite rows, each one a mausoleum for creatures that once stung, bit, bled.

Wolfgang stood there, alone. The boy didn't turn when the detective approached. Just spoke into the stillness.

"She kept saying she loved him," he said. "But it always sounded like she was auditioning."

St. John nodded. "Some people can't tell the difference between affection and performance. They think love's a mirror instead of a window."

Wolfgang looked up. "Will they charge her?"

"She's not walking," St. John said. "She knew what she was doing. That vial, the venom, the questions… she stitched it all together with mascara and lies."

The boy nodded slowly. "Then it's over."

"Nothing's over," St. John said. "Not really. There will be a trial. There will be attention you and your siblings do not want. Her defense team will no doubt try to cast suspicion on your mother, as she most certainly attempted to do by making it happen at the museum with your mother onsite."

He looked around. The museum was empty now, but it didn't feel quiet. It felt like it was listening.

Later, a few blocks away at the Elgin Street Diner, with its brightly lit vinyl booths and a server who poured coffee like it was penance, St. John sat with his thoughts. Outside, the neon "Always Open" sign buzzed faintly. A television in the corner played news clips from the fundraiser—footage of guests smiling, toasting, unaware. The broadcast then shifted to a montage of photographs of Brittany Omen.

St. John took a slow sip of his coffee, well aware that Brittany Omen might have gotten exactly what she wanted. here's a cruel irony in how killers are remembered. Not the victims—they fade, become shadows stitched to the footnotes of someone else's story. But the killers, their names echo. They're etched into headlines, whispered on documentaries, repeated like incantations in living rooms and courtrooms and dark corners of the internet. They achieve, in death or disgrace, the kind of permanence most people spend lifetimes chasing. It's as if the act of destruction brands them into history, while the lives they took become abstractions—soft, blurred, and forgotten. In the end, it isn't justice that grants immortality. It's atrocity.

They would say she lost everything—her freedom, her marriage, her pristine Instagram brand—but Brittany never played by those rules. Not really. In the end, it wasn't about wealth or even control. It was about attention. It was always about being seen. Noticed. The kind of seeing that turns heads and headlines. A viral sting. A perfect scandal. Brittany wasn't just a black widow in a cocktail dress—she was an algorithm in heels, engineered to go off in a room full of cameras. And when Ted Omen hit the floor, breath gone and poison blooming beneath his skin, Brittany didn't just step into infamy—she walked into the only spotlight she ever truly craved.

Maybe, thought Detective St. John, remembering Brittany's last sentence, her laugh about being remembered, she didn't want money, or to get away with it, or love. She wanted followers.

Now her mugshot will circulate like a red carpet photo—shared, reshared, dissected, worshipped. She will trend. She will be talked abouton true crime podcasts. She will exist, finally, in a way that feels permanent. And in the twisted logic of the age, that makes her a success.

Because fame, even the rotten kind, doesn't rot. It recycles.

Outside, the city kept humming its tired tune. Ottawa is good at this kind of forgetting—the kind that wears a suit and signs a condolence letter. The museum was clean again. The files were filed. The police tape was pulled down. What happened was "under review," which meant it had already been buried in triplicate. A legal drama would, in some months, ensue, one that would provide Brittany a number

Social media screams while government whispers. Brittany Omen's reels play beside news clips of ministers denying knowledge. A perfect harmony. The apps serve airbrushed delusion; the House of Commons serves procedural deflections. One looped lie leads into the next. The stories aren't that different. They just use different fonts.

There's something about the quiet in this city—something damp and cold and smug. The kind of silence that settles in parliamentary hallways and gleams in polished marble. Bureaucracy here is a taxidermy of ethics—

stuffed, posed, and glassy-eyed. Nobody wants the truth. They want a narrative that matches the optics. Brittany knew that. She played it like a violin.

Raymond Chandler once said the streets were dark with something more than night. In Ottawa, they're bright with lights, but every bulb casts a shadow

The detective stirred sugar into his cup and thought about Tatiana. About the look in her eyes when she said nothing, which was often more dangerous than when she spoke. He thought about the daughters—the triplets—and Wolfgang, who knew more about predators than any boy should.

He thought about the spider. About how something so small could unravel something so big.

Justice hadn't arrived with a bang. It had crawled in on eight legs, quiet and patient, and left its mark in the silence.

Back at the museum, under the moonlight's cold glow, a janitor swept the hall. The cases gleamed, wiped down, sanitized. But something had shifted. Something had entered the glasshouse that wouldn't leave.

Predators weren't just in the exhibits anymore.

They were in the story.

Chapter 14
Hall of Mirrors

The Elgin Street Courthouse loomed like a forgotten file folder, beige and blunt, squatting at the edge of downtown Ottawa. It had none of the neo-Gothic grandeur of Parliament Hill or the stately symmetry of Sussex Drive. No, this was a concrete ode to middle management—a monolith to the mid-twentieth century's most enduring legacy left in Ottawa: the massive public service and its bureaucratic shrug. The kind of building that looked like it apologized before you even walked in, not because it cared, but because it was procedure. Inside, the light was always fluorescent, the floors always buffed, the walls the color of policy briefs. It didn't echo so much as absorb sound—like any good bureaucracy should.

George waved his press badge at the security guard at the entrance, He didn't particularly care for courthouses, but he respected what they revealed. This one smelled faintly of disinfectant and anxiety. He descended the staircase to the pretrial detention cells, escorted by a bailiff who looked like he still used the term "typewriter" unironically.

In the basement, everything was colder. Not just the temperature—though it had that musty chill of recycled air—but in tone. Cement walls, metal benches, institutional blues and greys. This wasn't a place for redemption. It was a holding pattern.

And there she was. Brittany Omen—only that wasn't her name, not in here, where her fingerprints had revealed to police her earlier life.

"Crystal," she said, sitting with her hands folded in front of her. "My real name's Crystal. Crystal Haynes. I grew up in Windsor."

George raised an eyebrow. "That's quite the drop."

She smirked. "My mom was a stripper from Detroit. Crossed the river for a better life. Got pregnant. The guy took off faster than a TikTok trend. I bounced through foster homes like a glitchy reel. You can Google the rest—actually, wait, you will soon."

Her voice still had that performative lilt. George couldn't tell if she was confessing or auditioning.

"They found your record?" he asked, " I guess that's why they are holding you without bail?"

"Yep. Fingerprints at the museum. I've been Crystal all along. Surprise, I guess. Crown Attorney says that makes me a flight risk. That's not wrong. "

"And the fraud charges?"

"Decent list. Some identity stuff. A bit of wire fraud. Credit cards. Nothing that serious—well, unless you're a bank. To be honest, they never found about the best things I pulled off. But now I'm in for the real thing."
"You planned it?"

She tilted her head. "I mean, duh. It was a win-win. Either I got the money or I got famous. Either way, I was gonna *monetize the moment*. People forget the real crime is being irrelevant. The real tragedy is being forgotten."

George scribbled a note. She noticed and leaned forward, batting her eyes flirtatiously.

"Are you writing this down? Please make sure you spell my Insta handle right. I might lose followers in here, but the true fans always ride or die."

He didn't answer. Just closed his notebook.

As was his way, leaving the interview, George took a walk. He relished fresh air after talking to people. It wasn't a long walk in the rain, a few blocks south to the Elgin Street Diner. The booths were the same shade as blue legal aid folders and the coffee was strong enough to disbar you. George took a booth near the back.

From the corner, he saw someone familiar—Detective Clark St. John, hunched over a plate of eggs like they owed him answers. They made eye contact. A nod was exchanged. No words.

George stared out the window. The courthouse squatted in the distance, smugly surrounding its dusty paperwork. Hannah Arendt had it right—the Holocaust was orchestrated not by monsters but by men with ledgers. Evil didn't always wear jackboots. Sometimes it wore a lanyard.

He sipped his coffee. Crystal—Brittany—was a product of her time. Broken family, thirsty for the affirmation from social media to reflect her back to her as a perfect avatar of youth, wealth and beauty. . Justice as optics. The algorithm didn't care why you were trending, only that you were. He opened his notebook, toying with the idea of declining to write the story. Briefly. But deep down, he knew he would. this wasn't about judging. He wasn't a priest. He was a reporter. His job was to tell the truth, not decide who deserved a legacy.

With his pencil in one hand, coffee in the other, George began to write.

The story, after all, would sell. And Crystal, in her own sick way, had made her reflection unforgettable. Even if it was the kind of fame you couldn't scrub off in the shower.

Chapter 15
Requiem Under Glass

The cliffs above the Ottawa River were slick with rain, earning with their silhouettes the name of the neighbourhood, Rockcliffe. Park, along the shoreline. It was a light, ghostly rain, the kind that didn't fall in sheets but clung to every surface like memory. From the ribbon of road that was the Rockcliffe Parkway, the river below looked less like a landmark and more like a scar—deep, silvered, and cutting the land in half. Mist hung low, winding through the trees like a held breath. The evergreens dripped steadily; needles bowed. It was the kind of morning where nature grieved along with everyone else.

The funeral took place outdoors at Beechwood Cemetery, beneath a canopy of skeletal trees, beside a glass tombstone reading Ted Omen's name and the words, "Leader Entrepreneur, Innovator, Father" their leaves already thinned to black-gold ghosts. Ottawa's Beechwood Cemetery doesn't whisper. It broods.

Spread over a hill just east of downtown, Beechwood isn't just a cemetery—it's a memory trap. A place where the past lingers like pipe smoke in a parlour, thick and inescapable. The headstones lean into each other like old men at a pub, swapping war stories no one's quite sober enough to fact-check. The air tastes of iron and cedar. On a wet November day, with rain bleeding down the marble angels and the sky sagging low and grey, the place could talk you into believing that time is just a trick played on us by bureaucrats and priests.

They call it the National Cemetery of Canada now. That's the official line. But long before the plaques and ceremonial wreaths, Beechwood belonged to the forgotten. Irish navvies lie beneath the soil—names worn away, bones soaked with the mud of the Rideau Canal they died building. Their deaths were quiet. Not the kind with flags and anthems. Just accidents. Fever. Cold. A slip into water too dark to climb out of. The city never put those names on a wall. Beechwood did. In silence.

Come Remembrance Day a week from now, the brass buttons and stiff salutes will show up. Bugleswill echo off the tall oaks like ghosts refusing to fade. The soldiers get their rows now—clean, precise, with maple leaves etched into stone—but even their peace is unsettled. Because war doesn't end. It just gets recorded. And then rewritten. And then re-enacted in committee meetings and procurement contracts.

By this early November, day the leaves were mostly down, curled like burnt paper along the paths. The trees reached up with bare arms, stark against a sky the colour of gunmetal. The rain didn't fall hard, just persistently—like guilt. It streaked the tombstones, slicked the walkways, filled the engravings with water that looks too much like tears to mention aloud.

The living walk here like they're trying not to wake the dead.

But the truth is, Beechwood isn't sleeping. Not really.

It's watching. Waiting. Listening.

Because in a city built on orderly silence, this is one of the few places where the lies don't hold. The stories buried here are too heavy. Too real. And if you stand still long enough in the rain, one of them just might speak your name.

On this rainy afternoon, umbrellas bloomed like somber flowers among the mourners. The crowd stood on the rise, the green grass beneath their shoes slowly turning to mud. No music played. No one needed it. The rain composed its own elegy. Amongst the umbrellas a lone bare head stood tall above the crowd, and just below it a wrinkled trenchcoat. Detective St. John had decided to attend.

Tatiana Goode-Omen stood in the front, the wind tugging at the edge of her coat. Her scarf was pinned at the throat, her boots sunk half an inch into the soft earth. The triplets—Freya, Ariadne, and Erinye—stood close to her, their Ivy League glamour dulled into monochrome, eyes shadowed not just by grief but by knowledge. They had known this day would come. Just not like this.

Wolfgang stood a few feet back, alone in posture but not in presence. He looked older than seventeen in that moment. Not by the lines on his face, but by the weight in his eyes. A weight born of venom and loss and clarity no boy should have.

No one mentioned his second wife.

No one needed to.

The clutch of journalists and television cameras at the cemetery gates were reminder enough of her. A smattering of signs, limpid in the rain, their bright pink smeared by its drops, bore the hashtag "FreeBrittany. Her presence was felt.

The minister kept the service brief. A few words about public service, perseverance, legacy. All true, in part. But it was Wolfgang who stepped forward when the silence fell. The boy's dress shoes were muddy by the time he reached the podium placed over the open grave.

"My father," he began, voice clear in the cold air, "was not a perfect man. We all know that. But perfection isn't something we find in nature. We find liveliness; we find creativity, we find sparks. My father had all of those."

He looked at his mother. At his sisters. At the crowd.

"I remember when he and my mom worked side by side. Before the suits, before the speeches. Back when they stood on picket lines together. When they marched with signs and megaphones, not just bank accounts. I remember being a child and thinking the world was small enough to fix. Because they told me it could be."

He paused, drawing breath.

"He taught us to sort our recycling, to respect the rivers, to understand ecosystems—biological and political. He taught me the difference between an insect that bites and one that waits. Between predators and survivors."

Tatiana's eyes shimmered, but she remained still.

"He was not always kind," Wolfgang continued. "He made mistakes. But when I think of him, I choose to remember the man who pulled garbage from the riverbank, not the one who got lost in power and plastic. I remember the dad who made jokes about daddy longlegs, the one who showed me how to make a fire."

He folded the paper in his hand but didn't read from it. "He and my mom were idealists once. Maybe they still are. Maybe that's the legacy—the parts of us that still believe we can make things better, even when it's hard. Even when it hurts. I look over at my sisters' faces, and I see my own. In our eyes and our facial features, there, our parents are still together."

He stepped down. No applause. Just silence.

The casket was lowered. The soil waited.

Afterward, the mourners drifted away. Some returned to government offices. Environment Minister Jones-Middleton closed his umbrella, shook it out, and stepped swiftly into his waiting limosine. Marieve Dumont and Max Springhill left arm in arm, huddled together against the November chill. The protesters stayed longer, taking selfies in the rain, crafting curated posts about loss and resilience. One or two to an early drink. After noting the size of the protest crowd size, and the wording of their signes, George Jeremiah tucked his notebook into his raincoat, hunched his shoulders, and set off for the long walk back downtown, a walk which would take him past the Rideau Falls.

The Omen children stayed behind with their mother. They stood together in the rain until the workers began to cover the grave. No one spoke. The bonds between them didn't need narration.

Ted Omen had lived large, lived well and also badly, loved poorly, and died strangely. But like everyone else, he left behind something human. Something flawed, and still worth remembering.

Tatiana slipped her arm around Wolfgang's shoulders.
"We're still here," she whispered.
He nodded. "We are."

Legacy wasn't clean. It wasn't curated. It was compost—messy, organic, sometimes fertile. And when they walked down the path, the five of them together, their silhouettes blurred by mist, they weren't looking back.

Some distance off, Detective St. John stood, waiting. He had Tatiana's number. He would not speak to her on this day, but her resolved, looking at her flashing eyes, gentle but sharp, that he would be giving her a call.

The dead don't get rewrites.Only the living do.

About the Author

56

Cassandra Knight is a novelist, lawyer, and mother to four children.

www.ingramcontent.com/pod-product-compliance
Lightning Source LLC
Chambersburg PA
CBHW051107300726

48981CB00001B/27